anyth

D1107185

GRACIE
La Roo
AT PIG JUBILEE
written by MARSHA QUALEY
illustrated by KRISTYNA LITTEN
PICTURE WINDOW BOOKS
a capstone imprint

Gracie LaRoo at Pig Jubilee is published by
Picture Window Books, a Capstone imprint
1710 Roe Crest Drive
North Mankato, MN 56003
www.mycapstone.com

Library of Congress Cataloging-in-Publication data is available on the Library of Congress website.

Summary: Gracie has to learn to concentrate to help her team win the gold medal at the Pig Jubilee.

ISBN 978-1-5158-1442-9 (library binding)
ISBN 978-1-5158-1446-7 (ebook pdf)

Designer: Aruna Rangarajan

Editor: Megan Atwood

Production Specialist: Steve Walker

Printed and bound in the USA
010401F17

TABLE OF CONTENTS

GRACIE and the

NAME: Gracie LaRoo

TEAM: Water Sprites

CLAIM TO FAME:
Being the youngest pig to join a world-renowned synchronized swimming team!

SIGNATURE MOVE:
"When Pigs Fly" Spin

LIKES: Purple, clip-on tail bows, mud baths, new-mown hay smell

DISLIKES: Too much attention, doing laundry, scary movies

QUOTE

"I just hope I can be the kind of synchronized swimmer my team needs!"

WATER SPRITES

JINI

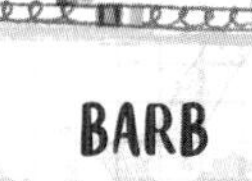

JIA

SU

MARTHA

SILVIA

The 25TH PIG JUBILEE
SYNCHRONIZED SWIMMING DIVISION

A BIG SPLASH

Gracie LaRoo was in the air. She held her breath and began the spin.

Once around.

Twice around.

One of the Pig Jubilee banners fluttered over the pool. Gracie tilted her head ever so slightly…

Gracie let out a long, bubbly moan underwater.

She had failed again.

When she couldn't hold her breath another moment, she kicked her way to the surface, where the other members of the team waited.

Jini, the captain of the Water Sprites, said, "You never miss four times in a row! What's wrong?"

Gracie said, "I was distracted by a banner."

Su said, “A banner? I know this is your first time in a world competition, Gracie, but champions don’t get distracted by banners.”

“Champions have to concentrate,” said Martha. “We need you at your best, Gracie.”

Silvia checked the clock. “That’s all we can do. Another team needs the pool.”

Jini walked into the locker room with Gracie. "We can win tomorrow if everyone does her job. You could be the youngest water ballet swimmer to ever win a Jubilee gold medal, Gracie! You know what you have to do."

Gracie knew. She had to focus. She had to concentrate. She would not let her team down.

Chapter 2
Swimming Star

Some of the Sprites started arguing about what to have for dinner. As she dressed, Gracie thought, *They are angry because they are worried, and it's all my fault. I have to do better.*

Gracie raced out, the first to leave the locker room.

She found a chair in a corner of the building. She pulled a notebook out of her bag, curled up, and studied the team's routine.

She knew the routine by heart. But she read through it again and again. She could see every step in her mind like a slow-motion movie.

The Razzle

Dazzle Ring.

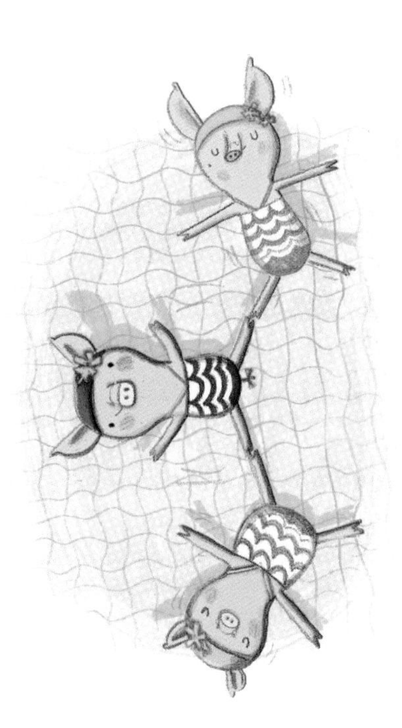

The Wiggly

Piggly Pyramid.

The Sooey,

Sooey Star.

And the grand

finale: A Pig Flies.

That was Gracie's special spin. Three times around.

She closed her eyes and whispered, "I will not let the team down." She clutched the notebook to her heart. "I will concentrate."

When she opened her eyes a tall sow was standing right there.

Gracie gasped and then said, "Marie Franswa!"

Marie was captain of the Aqua Stars team and the most famous water ballet swimmer in the world. Her team had won gold medals at the last three Jubilees.

"And I know who you are," Marie said. "Gracie LaRoo of the Water Sprites. I hear you have been winning many medals in your country."

Gracie put her notebook in the bag. She pulled out her camera. “Could I please have a picture?”

“Of course, but let us go outside,” said Marie. “I photograph best in natural light.”

Marie gave Gracie a warm smile.

"How do you like Pig Jubilee?" she asked as she posed.

"It's exciting to see so many athletes from around the world," said Gracie. "But I'm trying not to be distracted."

She looped the camera around her neck and clicked a final picture. "Did you ever feel that way?"

"Of course!" said Marie. "My first time here I was so excited my head was spinning!"

She gave Gracie's shoulder a quick poke. "I must join my team for practice. Good luck, little piglet." Then she winked. "But not too much luck. I want to win!"

CONCENTRATE!

After Marie was gone Gracie looked around. *Where was her bag?*

Then she remembered: She had left it inside by the chair.

An athlete in a warm-up suit was asleep in the chair where Gracie had been reading her notebook.

She peeked behind his bag. She peeked behind the chair.

No purple bag.

Gracie leaned against the wall. Her swimsuits, caps, and snout clips were in that bag. Everything she needed for the gold medal competition the next day was gone!

"Oh no," Gracie cried. "My notebook!"

Then she had a horrible thought. Had Marie taken it when she went back inside?

Were she and the Aqua Stars reading the notebook right now? Would they have time to learn one of the Sprites' special moves?

Gracie wailed. "Why did I get distracted?" She had to find out if the Aqua Stars had her bag. She walked as quickly as she to the locker room.

Once she arrived, Gracie tiptoed in. She wasn't supposed to go inside when another team was practicing. So Gracie looked for her bag everywhere as fast as she could.

The empty room echoed with sounds from the pools.

Suddenly, someone said, "What are you doing?"

One of the Aqua Stars walked toward her from the showers.

"You're not allowed in here." She opened a door and yelled,

"We have a spy! She has a camera!"

The other Stars rushed in.

Gracie said, "I'm not spying! I'm looking for my bag. Someone took it."

"And you thought one of us stole it?" Marie said. "Never! We would never do that. Am I right, girls?" Seven heads bobbed up and down.

"We must practice," Marie said, "and you must go."

Gracie slunk out of the locker room. She was so embarrassed.

Nearby, a team came out of another locker room. "Let's go to the hotel," someone said.

Gracie thought, *The hotel! I bet one of the Sprites saw my bag and took it. I bet it's in the room right now.*

She raced to the hotel.

She burst into the team's room, panting.

No purple bag.

THE GOLD MEDAL

Gracie was so mad she tore off her bow and threw it down on a bed. "It's not by the chair, it's not in the locker room, and the team didn't bring it back to the room. Where is my bag?"

Her yelling was loud. Gracie hugged herself, took a deep breath, and said, "Calm down."

She said, "Concentrate."

She lay on her bed. *When you lose something,* she thought, *where can you go to find it?*

Then Gracie thumped her head with a hoof. "Why didn't I think of that first?"

A bristled boar stood behind the Lost and Found counter.

"Did someone turn in a purple bag?" Gracie asked him. "It has the name *Gracie* in pink glitter."

The boar dropped the bag on the counter.

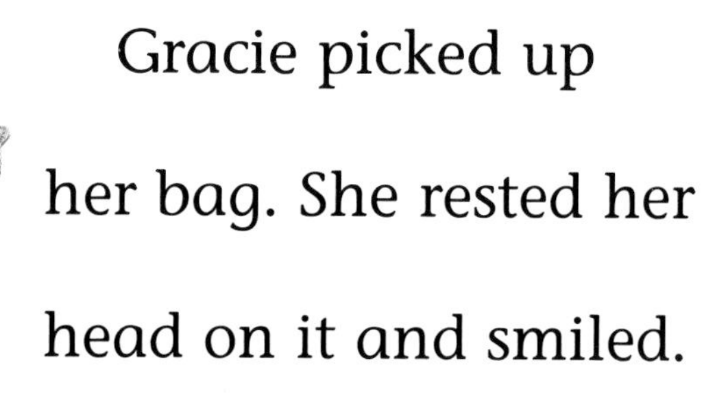

Gracie picked up her bag. She rested her head on it and smiled.

The next day, at the competition, Gracie LaRoo was in the air spinning.

Concentrating.

Once around.

Twice around.

Three perfect spins!

After the performance, the Water Sprites crowded onto the platform.

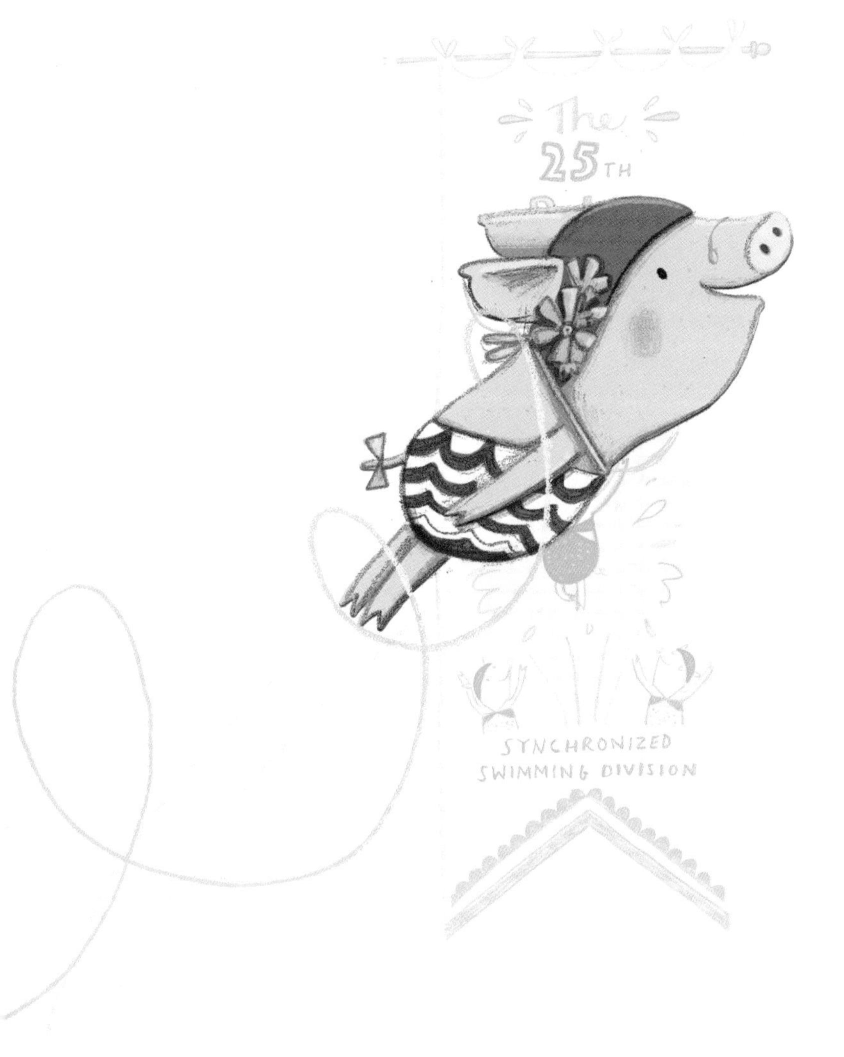

They had won the event!

As Gracie kissed her gold medal, she felt a tug on her tail.

Marie Franswa hugged her.

A silver medal hung from her neck. “Congratulations, Gracie,” Marie said. The rest of the Aqua Stars congratulated her too.

Before Gracie could reply, she felt her teammates lift and throw her high into the air.

She couldn’t be prouder. The Water Sprites were champions at Pig Jubilee!

JUBILEE
GRACIE
WATERS
9.0
9.2
9.8
10.0

GLOSSARY

banner — a large sign

bristle — stiff hair

champion — someone who wins at something

competition — two or more teams trying to win at something

concentrate — to focus on something

distracted — to have a hard time focusing on one thing

flutter — to move back and forth quickly

slunk — to have moved away with the hope no one noticed

TALK ABOUT IT!

1. Have you ever had a hard time concentrating? How did you get your concentration back?

2. Have you been on a team? Talk about a time when you felt like the team counted on you.

3. How did Gracie find her bag? What did she need to do?

WRITE ABOUT IT!

1. Write a letter from Gracie to her teammates. What would Gracie say to her teammates before the competition in the Jubilee?

2. Pretend you are a reporter covering the event. Write a news story about the Water Sprites and Gracie's performance.

3. What was it like to be one of Gracie's teammates? Write a story from that point of view.

Marsha Qualey is the author of many books for readers young and old. Though she learned to swim when she was very young, she says she has never tried any of the moves and spins Gracie does so well.

Marsha has four grown-up children and two grandchildren. She lives in Wisconsin with her husband and their two non-swimming cats.

About the Illustrator

Kristyna Litten is an award winning children's book illustrator and author. After studying illustration at Edinburgh College of Art, she now lives and works from Yorkshire in the UK, with her pet rabbit Herschel.

Kristyna would not consider herself a very good swimmer as she can only do the breaststroke, but when she was younger, she would do a tumble roll and a handstand in the shallow end of the pool.

THE WONDERFUL, THE AMAZING, THE PIG-TASTIC GRACIE LAROO!

Discover more at
www.capstonekids.com

- Find out more about Gracie and her adventures.
- Follow the Water Sprites as they craft their routines.
- Figure out what you would do . . . if you were the awesome Gracie LaRoo!